To Sterling and Nettie Green,
who heard The People singing

And with special thanks to
Chief Kenneth S. Clark, Sr., Odette Wright, and the Nanticoke Dance Troupe
—BJM

Special thanks to the Comfort family
—TLWD

 Inquiries should be addressed to
Lothrop, Lee & Shepard Books, a division of William Morrow & Company, Inc.,
1350 Avenue of the Americas, New York, New York 10019.
Printed in Singapore.
First Edition 1 2 3 4 5 6 7 8 9 10
Library of Congress Cataloging in Publication Data
Mitchell, Barbara. *Red Bird* / by Barbara Mitchell; illustrated by Todd L.W. Doney.
p. cm. Summary: Katie, also known as Red Bird, joins her family and other Indians at the annual powwow
in southern Delaware, where they celebrate their Nanticoke heritage with music, dancing, and special foods.
ISBN 0-688-10859-8. — ISBN 0-688-20860-1 (lib. bdg.)
1. Naticoke Indians—Rites and ceremonies—Juvenile fiction.
[1. Nanticoke Indians—Fiction. 2. Indians of North America—Fiction. 3. Powwows—Fiction.]
I. Doney, Todd, ill. II. Title. PZ7.M686Re 1996 [E]—dc20 95-9664 CIP AC

The illustrations in this book were done in oil paints on canvas. The display type was set in Caslon. The text was set
in ITC Novarese. Printed and bound by Tien Wah Press. Production supervision by Cliff Bryant.

Red Bird

Barbara Mitchell / Todd L.W. Doney

Lothrop, Lee & Shepard Books New York

Mom takes the regalia out of the trunk. Doeskin dresses, buckskin leggings, soft beaded moccasins, Katie's scarlet shawl. It's September, time for the Nanticoke powwow.

Dad loads the camper with cooking pots and blankets, drumsticks, rattles, and jingling bells. He places his feather headdress proudly on top of it all.

Off to the powwow they go. Away from screaming sirens and honking horns. Away from crowded buildings that scrape the city sky. Down past Dover Air Force Base, where jets roar over the camper like giant claps of thunder.

Suddenly they are in the country. Fields stretch flat and green as far as Katie can see. LIVE CRABS—HARD AND SOFT, roadside signs cry out.

"We're almost there," says Dad. He rolls down his window to breathe in bayside air.

"Long before the white man came, Nanticoke held their crab feasts. They fished the Delaware Bay."

Around by Nanticoke cornfields golden in the sun, the world is strangely quiet. There is nothing to be heard. Nothing but summer crickets chirping their good-byes. And from the distant pine trees, the beating of Nanticoke drums.

Down the sandy roadside, the drums call Katie's name: Red Bird, Red Bird, RED BIRD, RED BIRD. "Katie" fades away. She is Red Bird, Nanticoke Daughter. She hears her people singing. She hears the calling drums: Hurry, Red Bird, hurry! The powwow has begun.

Dad parks the camper deep in the fragrant pines. Grandma and Grandpa are there. And aunts and uncles and cousins, all the way from Canada. Grandpa scoops Red Bird into his arms. "Red Bird, you've come!"

Over in the arena, the Nanticoke chief takes his place. "The drumbeat is our heartbeat," Chief Red Deer says. He calls for all the dancers. "Nanticoke . . . Delaware . . . Rose Bud Sioux. Cherokee . . . Iroquois." The dancers enter from the east, like the rising sun.

Red Bird moves into the circle. Step-STEP, step-STEP. Step-STEP, step-STEP. The singing grows louder. The drumbeat grows stronger. Red Bird's heart beats with joy.

Dancing makes Red Bird hungry. Fry bread puffs and sizzles. "Honey on mine," says Mom. Dad smears his with butter. Red Bird chooses spicy beans.

Under rainbow-colored tents, traders show their wares. A Cherokee necklace? An Iroquois rattle, a turtle carved of bone? What shall Red Bird buy?

At last she decides. She must have the headband with N*anticoke* spelled out in tiny beads.

"Shawl dancers, take your places," Chief Red Deer calls.

Dipping, gliding, turning, fluttering her shawl like wings—she *is* Red Bird, wonderful creature, beautiful bird of the earth.

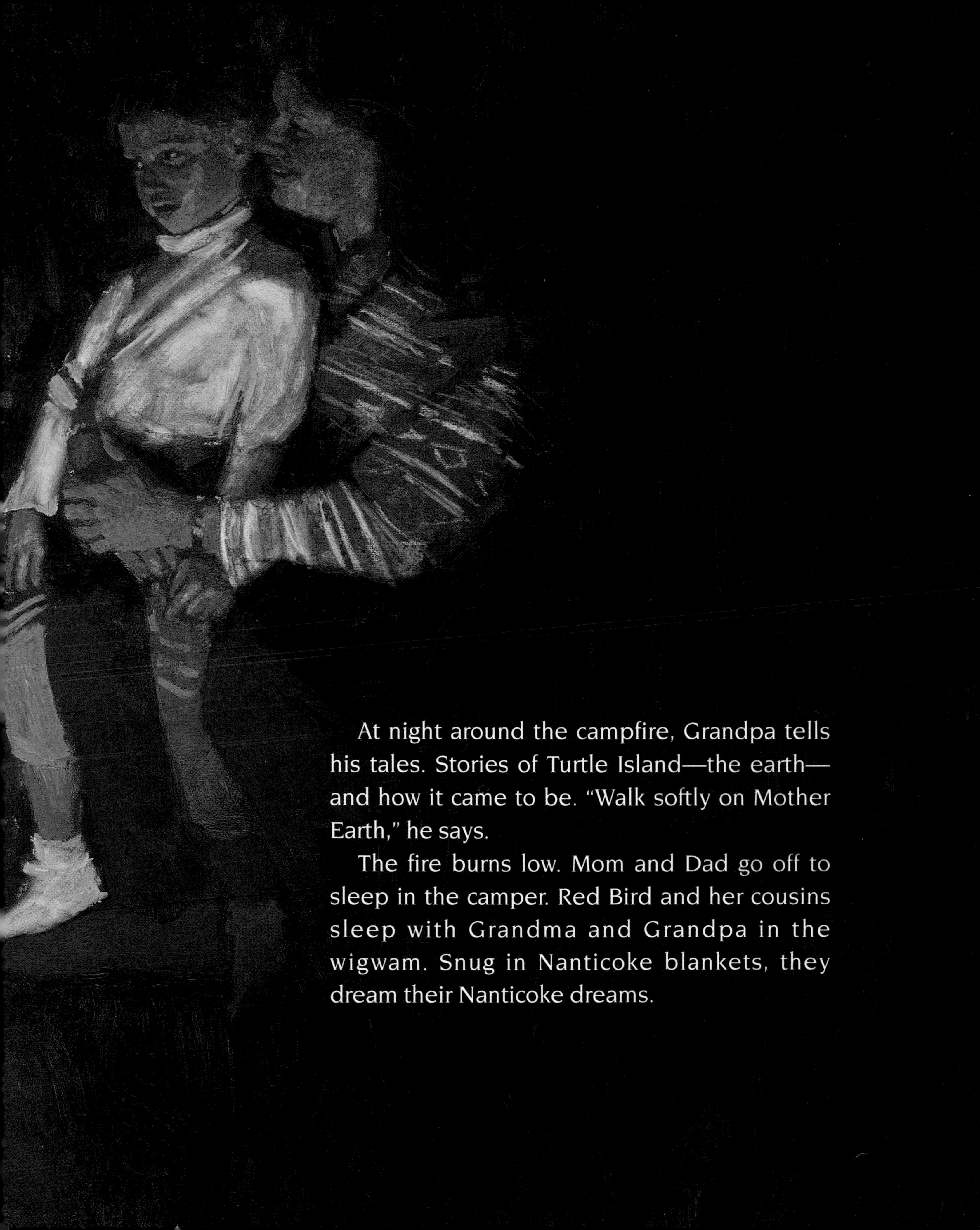

At night around the campfire, Grandpa tells his tales. Stories of Turtle Island—the earth—and how it came to be. "Walk softly on Mother Earth," he says.

The fire burns low. Mom and Dad go off to sleep in the camper. Red Bird and her cousins sleep with Grandma and Grandpa in the wigwam. Snug in Nanticoke blankets, they dream their Nanticoke dreams.

In the morning, the dancing and feasting begin again. Red Bird wishes the powwow could go on forever.

But all too soon it is time to pack up and go home. Red Deer calls for the final dance. "We dance the Round Dance—the dance of all peoples," the chief explains to the spectators. "Come, take hands and join in."

Red feet and white feet, black feet and yellow feet step to the beat of the heart. Then the dancers slip out to the west, like the setting sun. The drumbeat grows softer and softer: RED BIRD, RED BIRD, Red Bird, Red Bird. "Red Bird" fades away.

NANTICOKE

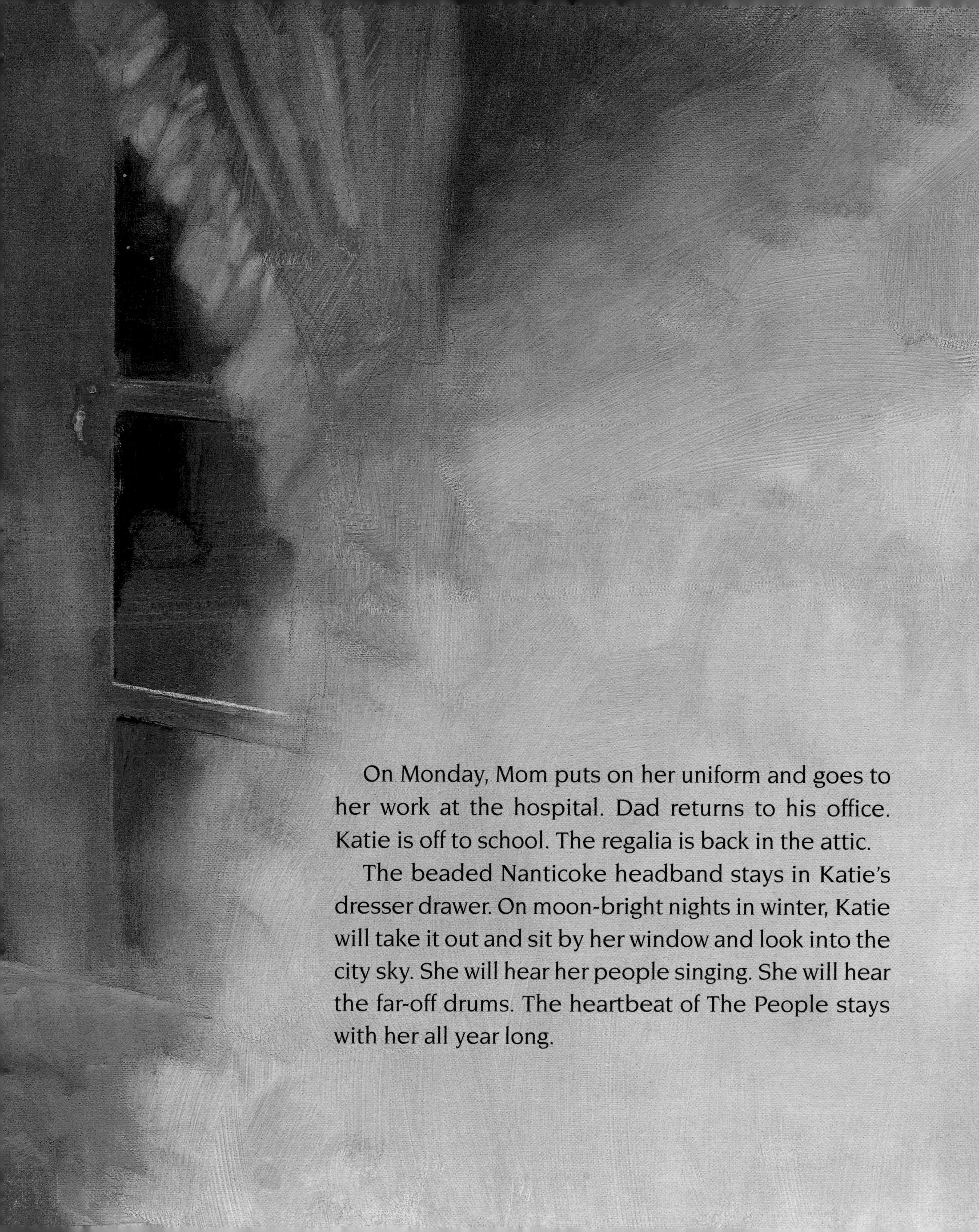

On Monday, Mom puts on her uniform and goes to her work at the hospital. Dad returns to his office. Katie is off to school. The regalia is back in the attic.

The beaded Nanticoke headband stays in Katie's dresser drawer. On moon-bright nights in winter, Katie will take it out and sit by her window and look into the city sky. She will hear her people singing. She will hear the far-off drums. The heartbeat of The People stays with her all year long.

AUTHOR'S NOTE

The Nanticoke are an Algonquian tribe that first lived along the shores of Chesapeake Bay. When laws made by European settlers made it difficult for these Native Americans to keep their identity, some of the Nanticoke moved to Canada. Others resettled in Delaware and New Jersey.

Today the majority of Nanticoke live in southern Delaware. Every September the Nanticoke Indian Association hosts a powwow. A powwow is a get-together, a time of celebration that preserves the heritage of the Nanticoke people and provides an opportunity for the reunion of families and for the renewal of bonds of friendship with both Indian and non-Indian friends.

The Nanticoke powwow is held on a farm near Millsboro, Delaware. Native Americans representing more than forty tribes from Florida to Canada and from as far west as North Dakota, Texas, and Oklahoma join in the singing, dancing, eating of Native American foods, and exhibition of crafts that characterize this festive occasion. Thousands of non-Indian spectators come to learn about Native American customs.